Dear Parents:

Congratulations! Your child is taking the first steps on an exciting journey. The destination? Independent reading!

STEP INTO READING® will help your child get there. The program offers five steps to reading success. Each step includes fun stories and colorful art or photographs. In addition to original fiction and books with favorite characters, there are Step into Reading Non-Fiction Readers, Phonics Readers and Boxed Sets, Sticker Readers, and Comic Readers—a complete literacy program with something to interest every child.

Learning to Read, Step by Step!

Ready to Read   Preschool–Kindergarten
• big type and easy words • rhyme and rhythm • picture clues
For children who know the alphabet and are eager to begin reading.

Reading with Help   Preschool–Grade 1
• basic vocabulary • short sentences • simple stories
For children who recognize familiar words and sound out new words with help.

Reading on Your Own   Grades 1–3
• engaging characters • easy-to-follow plots • popular topics
For children who are ready to read on their own.

Reading Paragraphs   Grades 2–3
• challenging vocabulary • short paragraphs • exciting stories
For newly independent readers who read simple sentences with confidence.

Ready for Chapters   Grades 2–4
• chapters • longer paragraphs • full-color art
For children who want to take the plunge into chapter books but still like colorful pictures.

STEP INTO READING® is designed to give every child a successful reading experience. The grade levels are only guides; children will progress through the steps at their own speed, developing confidence in their reading.

Remember, a lifetime love of reading starts with a single step!

© 2015 Viacom International Inc. All rights reserved. Published in the United States by Random House Children's Books, a division of Random House LLC, 1745 Broadway, New York, NY 10019, and in Canada by Random House of Canada Limited, Toronto, Penguin Random House Companies. Nickelodeon, Dora and Friends, and all related titles, logos, and characters are trademarks of Viacom International Inc.

Step into Reading, Random House, and the Random House colophon are registered trademarks of Random House LLC.

Visit us on the Web!
StepIntoReading.com
randomhousekids.com

Educators and librarians, for a variety of teaching tools, visit us at RHTeachersLibrarians.com

ISBN 978-0-553-52093-4 (trade) — ISBN 978-0-553-52094-1 (lib. bdg.)

Printed in the United States of America

10 9 8 7 6 5 4 3 2 1

nickelodeon

DORA
and
Friends™

Island of the Lost Horses

by Kristen L. Depken

based on the teleplay "Lost Horses"
by Valerie Walsh Valdes

illustrated by David Aikins

Random House 🏠 New York

One day, Dora and her
friends visit a farm.
They meet the farmer.

Naiya's cousin Marko
wants to ride
the farmer's horse!

Her name is Dulce.
There is a long line
of kids waiting
to ride her.

The farmer's other
horses are lost.
They are on the island
of lost horses.

Dulce whinnies.
She wants Dora
to follow her.
She runs off!

The farmer gives Dora

a magic necklace.

It matches

Dulce's necklace!

Dora and her friends
follow Dulce's tracks.
They find Dulce
on a raft.

The raft takes the
friends through a fog.
They arrive on the
island of lost horses!

The magic necklaces
start to glow.
The lost horses
are near!

The friends search
for the horses.
Dora and Naiya run.
Marko gets
to ride Dulce.

The horses are found!
Dulce is happy
to see her friends.

Oh, no!
Bandits are coming!
They want to steal
the horses!

Dora tells the horses
to run fast.
The bandits chase them!

The friends lead the horses onto the raft.

At the raft, Dora's
necklace glows.
Dulce is stuck!

The bandits are coming!
Marko and Dora
ride to Dulce.
They reach her
just in time!

Dora frees Dulce.

They ride to the raft.

Dulce leaps on!

Everyone is safe.

Dora and her friends
take the horses
back to the farm.
The farmer is
very happy!

The farmer lets Dora
keep the magic necklace.

Dora will always be
a special friend
to Dulce
and the lost horses.